For Stephen and Dee – SG

For Okikiade and Iyun-Ade – ET

Text copyright © 2004 by Sally Grindley
Illustrations copyright © 2004 by Eleanor Taylor

Published by Bloomsbury, New York and London
Distributed to the trade by Holtzbrinck Publishers
Printed in Hong Kong/China

Library of Congress Cataloging-in-Publication Data available upon request
ISBN 1 58234 882 0

First U.S. Edition 2004

1 3 5 7 9 10 8 6 4 2

Bloomsbury USA Children's Books
175 Fifth Avenue
New York, NY 10010

All papers used by Bloomsbury Publishing are natural, recyclable products made from
wood grown in well-managed forests. The manufacturing processes conform
to the environmental regulations of the country of origin.

A Little Bit of Trouble

by Sally Grindley
illustrated by Eleanor Taylor

BLOOMSBURY
CHILDREN'S
BOOKS

We're ready, my little bears.
I've packed the sandwiches,
chocolates and cakes so
off we go ...

It's a beautiful day for a picnic. The sun is shining, the sky is blue and it's so peaceful here in the countryside.

Ha! I used to do that myself when I was young. Just make sure you close the gate behind you. We don't want the nasty old bull chasing us.

Don't run too far ahead,
my little bears. Grandpa
isn't as young as he was.

Here's a perfect spot. A nice shady tree to keep off the sun and a little river running by.

These sandwiches are delicious, but silly Grandpa must have left the cakes behind. My memory's not as good as it was.

Let's all have a little
doze in the sun, then
we'll play hide-and-seek.

Ouch! Who's throwing things? Squirrels
I expect. They can be quite mischievous.
Now where are those bears?

Oh goodness! Help! Run, little bears, run!

Stay where you are,
little bears, while
Grandpa shoos the
nasty old bull away.

Thank goodness he's gone. What sensible bears you are to hide up a tree! Your mother will be so pleased when I tell her.

Time to go home now, I think.

It's been such a perfect day, apart from our little bit of trouble.